D1575095

For Ida

20066513

MORAY COUNCIL
LIBRARIES &
INFORMATION SERVICES
JA

This edition first published in 2000 by
Cat's Whiskers
96 Leonard Street
London EC2A 4XD

ISBN 1 90301 216 3 (hbk)
ISBN 90301 217 1 (pbk)

Originally published in Belgium by Uitgeverij Clavis, Hasselt, 2000
Copyright © Uitgeverij Clavis, Hasselt, 2000
English text copyright © Cat's Whiskers 2000

A CIP catalogue record for this book is available from the British Library

All rights reserved. Without limiting the rights under copyright reserved above, no part of this
publication may be reproduced, stored in or introduced into a retrieval system, or transmitted, in
any form or by any means (electronic, mechanical, photocopying, recording or otherwise), without
the prior written permission of both the copyright owner and the above publisher of the book.

Printed in Belgium

Flop-Ear and Annie

Guido Van Genechten

CAT'S Whiskers

This is Flop-Ear...

... and this is Annie.

Every day Flop-Ear watched as Annie played. She was so clever: she could juggle with three balls, and sing while she skipped.

Flop-Ear day-dreamed about Annie
being his friend. He imagined
the two of them
playing together.
What fun they
would have...

But Annie never seemed to notice Flop-Ear,
and he didn't dare speak to her.
She probably thinks I'm stupid,
he said to himself.

Maybe my trousers are too short -
real rabbits wear LONG trousers.

The next day Flop-Ear shuffled past Annie's
house - in long trousers.
Annie tried hard not to laugh.

Maybe she thinks
I'm not strong enough,
said Flop-Ear.
He marched past her
with square shoulders.

Annie didn't seem impressed.

Perhaps it's because I don't look clever enough, thought Flop-Ear. So he put on his grandfather's glasses.

Maybe she wants a friend with lots of carrots...

Or one with handsome brown spots...

Or perhaps she'd prefer
a mystery friend,
one with secrets
to share.

But when Annie saw the mystery costume,
she ran away screaming.
"Don't be scared," shouted Flop-Ear,
"it's only me!"
But Annie was so frightened, she kept
on running until she tripped over a branch.

Flop-Ear caught up with her
and took off his mask.
Annie started to laugh.
"Flop-Ear!" she cried. "It was you!"
"Y-e-e-s..." Flop-Ear was
a bit embarrassed.

Then he became very serious.
"Annie," he asked, "would you ... um
would you like to go for a walk
with me tomorrow?"
"I'd love to," said Annie,
"as long as you don't
wear your mask!"
They both started
to giggle.
"You're so much
nicer the way
you are!"

The next day Flop-Ear arrived at
the meeting place much too early.
Will she come, he asked himself.
Then he noticed two small,
fluffy ears in the distance.
"Annie!" he shouted,
and ran towards her.

He gave Annie a little blue parcel
tied up with string:
"For you," he said.
"How lovely! A chain
of carrots! They're
my favourites!"
cried Annie.
"Mine too,"
replied Flop-Ear.

Together they walked
through the wood. The birds
were singing loudly, and
Annie's paw felt very soft
when Flop-Ear held it.
It was so good to have
a friend.